LOST

LOST

SHARON JENNINGS

HIP Xtreme Novels

NATIONAL LIBRARY OF CANADA CATALOGUING IN PUBLICATION DATA
Jennings, Sharon
    Lost / Sharon Jennings.

ISBN 978-1-926847-21-4

    I. Title.

PS8569.E563L67 2012   jC813'.54   C2012-901225-4

General editor: Paul Kropp
Text Design: Laura Brady
Illustrations by: Charlie Hnatiuk
Cover design: Robert Corrigan

1 2 3 4 5 6 7   17 16 15 14 13 12

Printed and bound in Canada

High Interest Publishing acknowledges the financial support of the
Government of Canada through the Canada Book Fund for our
publishing activities.

Rafe thought it would be easy to be a counsellor at a wilderness camp. But when young Matt Phillips heads off into the woods, both young men become lost. Then it's a fight for survival – against the woods and against each other – just to stay alive.

Contents

Chapter 1

Eat, Drink and Be Merry

They could all see the accident now. The boys crammed onto the seats at the left side of the bus, shoving each other for a better view. Even Rafe stood up from his seat. He couldn't help himself. He had to look, too.

The car had been totalled. The front bumper was smashed into the back seat, glass all over the highway. No way anyone survived that. But where was the other car?

Then Rafe saw it – not a car, a moose. The huge animal was torn apart, a gaping hole where the chest should be. The antlers were ripped from its head and lay near the ditch. The hind legs twisted the wrong way, and the front legs were missing.

Rafe watched the firefighters hose blood off the highway. Black crows circled overhead, waiting their turn.

The boys on the bus laughed and pointed. "Cool!" "Gross!" Many of them had phones up, snapping photos.

Rafe turned away, disgusted with himself for even looking. *Someone died here. An animal was slaughtered here. What's wrong with us that we all stare at this?*

But then he realized not all the kids were looking at the accident. One kid was still in his seat, a kid named Matt, biting his fingers. The kid was quietly rocking back and forth.

Rafe moved up the aisle and sat beside him. "You okay?" he asked.

Matt didn't turn around, just nodded.

But Rafe saw that the kid was white and sweating. He knew what to say. "Put your head down," he ordered. "Take deep breaths."

"Leave me alone."

"Hey, buddy. I'm your counsellor for the next week. You have to listen to me. And I know what I'm doing. If you feel sick, put your head down."

Matt didn't look at Rafe, but he put his head down.

"It's no big deal, you know," Rafe added. "I'm not feeling too good myself after looking at that mess."

"Hey! What's wrong with Doormat?" a kid yelled.

Suddenly, twenty guys were watching.

Rafe thought fast and dropped down to the floor. "Here it is!" Rafe called out as he stood up. Then he glared at the other kids. "What are you staring at? Matt just dropped his . . . ah . . . wallet."

Matt pulled himself up. "Thanks," he mumbled. He pretended to shove something in his pocket

"Forget it."

The boys were ordered back to their seats and the bus began to roll. The group leader spoke into the mic. "We should arrive at camp in an hour," he said. "Sorry for the delay, but you learn to expect this sort of thing in the north country."

Rafe went to sit with the other counsellors in the back row of the bus. He saw a couple of boys grinning at Matt. Something in the way they looked, something in their eyes . . . wasn't right. So Rafe got up again and went to sit beside Matt.

"Want to tell me about it?" he asked.

Matt shrugged. "Nothing to tell. You heard them."

"Doormat? That what you mean?"

"One of those jerks goes to my school. Guess he's been talking to the others." Matt tugged his jacket collar up around his neck and twisted away.

Rafe tried to remember what he had read about this kid. Matthew Henson. Lived with a grandmother. No money. Went to school hungry most days. Arrested a couple of times for little stuff. Hand-picked by the Kids Count Program for this northern camp.

Rafe thought about his own life. Big house, cars, money. Great parents. Lots of trips and toys. The best of everything, including his girlfriend, Diana. Just thinking about her did things to him. Rafe shifted in his seat. Better focus on the coming week, he told himself. A week with a bunch of mouthy young offenders in the woods. That should take his mind off Diana.

The bus slowed and made a right turn off the highway. There was a long, bumpy stretch of gravel road and then, ten minutes later, Camp Hope. Some kids pumped fists in the air. Then they grabbed knapsacks and jackets, pushing each other to get off.

The cold air was a shock after the stuffy heat of the bus. Rafe zipped up his coat and silently thanked his mom for making him take the winter parka. "Don't argue with me," she had said. "I know it's April, but there will still be ice on the lake at Camp Hope."

When he got back, he'd let her know she was right. She'd like that.

Mr. Longo was there to welcome them. "We've got a great week planned, boys, whatever the weather. You were all assigned a bunkhouse and a counsellor back in the city. Go with your counsellor. The bunkies are down that path. Get settled in, and supper's in twenty minutes in the main hall." He waved at a building behind him.

Rafe walked with Matt and his three other boys to cabin five. Inside were two bunk beds and a single bed near the window. There was a sleeping bag and pillow on each mattress.

A kid named Yossi jumped on the single bed. "First dibs," he shouted. "This one's mine!"

Rafe shook his head. "Get your stinkin' butt off my bed. You guys get the bunks. Any arguments over who gets top or bottom?"

"Doormat should be on the floor," a short kid named Jake said. "He pees himself, and I'm not sleeping downwind of that."

The others all laughed. Rafe glanced at Matt, who acted as if he hadn't heard. No matter. Rafe spun round and took Jake by the collar. "No. Not going to happen. Not on my watch."

"Hey! Chill, man! It was a joke."

Rafe pushed Jake and let go. The kid stumbled and fell against a bed frame. Then Rafe looked at Matt. "And you. What's the matter with you? Stand up for yourself." He glared at Matt, and then at the others. There was a moment of silence, a moment when anything might happen. One kid might shove another, or say something, or do something and then. . . .

Then the gong sounded.

"Supper," Rafe announced. "Come on. Let's all eat, drink and be merry."

Three boys shoved to get out the door and rushed along the path. They were all following the light back to the main hall. But Matt lagged behind.

Rafe waited.

Matt smiled at him, but there was nothing friendly about it. Then he repeated Rafe's words. "Eat, drink and be merry. But you forgot the rest. The rest goes like this – for tomorrow . . . tomorrow we die."

Chapter 2

Moaning in the Night

In the main hall, there was dinner and a movie. And then lots of pep talks.

Mr. Longo told them how crappy his life was until he turned it around. How he went back to school and got a good job. Then he asked each counsellor to say something. Three of them had been to this camp and had returned to help out. Their lives had been messed up, and they fixed them. Here, starting at this camp.

Rafe felt like a fraud. What could he say? *I'm a rich kid and feel sorry for you suckers? I have everything and want to throw a few crumbs your way? I need this gig on my résumé. All true, but. . . .*

It was Rafe's turn. The kids were watching him.

Some smiled, others stared with a hard look in their eyes.

"Every person deserves a chance," Rafe said. "Every person deserves the right to try. No one deserves a rotten life. I've been lucky, that's all. But it doesn't . . . you know . . . seem fair."

Lame.

The evening ended and Mr. Longo sent the kids to the bathhouse before lights out. Then he spoke to the counsellors.

"First night. Could get rough," Mr. Longo said. "Some of these kids might actually be homesick – who knows why, coming from their so-called homes. And some will want to take you on. Be prepared. Sleep with one eye open. And here." He handed out whistles. "Anything goes down, blow like your life depends on it." He grinned. "It just might."

Rafe remembered Matt. The kid had said, "For tomorrow we die." Rafe shivered. He hung the whistle around his neck and made sure it was tied tightly.

The counsellors stepped outside. The temperature had dropped and they could see their breath make steam in the air. Rafe wasn't surprised to see soft flakes of snow drifting down. They wished each other

good luck.

An older counsellor touched Rafe's arm. "One word of advice," he whispered. "Don't let them get away with anything. It's all alpha-dog in this place. And you've got to be top dog."

Rafe tried to think of himself as an alpha dog, the leader of a pack. Maybe he could pull it off. Maybe.

"Shout, threaten, look tough. And mean it."

Rafe nodded, then started down his path. He hadn't

gone far when Mr. Longo called him back.

"I've known your dad a long time," Mr. Longo said. "He gave me a break years ago when I first got out of jail."

Rafe knew the story.

"So when he asked, I said sure. I'd give you this job. But Rafe. . . ." Mr. Longo leaned in close. "Don't screw up. These boys need a strong leader, not some rich kid having fun."

"Yes sir. I know. I won't let you down."

Mr. Longo grunted. Then he turned abruptly and shut the hall door.

Rafe huddled into his parka and moved down the path. He breathed in the clean sharp air and tilted his head back to stare into the dark. He could hear the wind in the trees over his head. White pines. The real thing – the real old-growth forest of the north. The wind moaned and groaned and sent little flicks of fear down his spine. Then it stopped. Suddenly the world was quiet and still.

Except for a low moaning sound.

It wasn't the wind.

It was human.

Rafe held his breath and listened. The groaning

was coming from the bathhouse.

Rafe turned and ran as quickly as he could over the tree roots. He swung open the door and flicked on the light. Nothing. Then he heard the scrape of a boot on tile.

Quickly he moved from stall to stall, pulling open every door until he found the source of the groaning.

It was Matt. The kid was tied to a toilet, a washcloth stuck in his mouth, his pants down around his feet.

Chapter 3

Doormat?

Rafe felt fury push up inside his gut. Quickly he untied Matt and pulled the cloth from his mouth. He turned away, expecting the kid to fix his pants.

But Matt didn't move.

"Come on, Matt. Pull up your pants. Then we'll talk."

The kid still didn't move.

"I'll get Mr. Longo," Rafe said.

That did it. "No!" Matt leaned down and tugged up his jeans. "Why don't you just leave me here? As soon as nobody's looking, this is where I'll end up. I always do. So . . . I'll make it easy for everybody and spend the week in the can."

The anger Rafe felt for the other kids turned toward Matt. "What's wrong with you? Why'd you let them do this to you?" The words were wrong. Rafe knew it as soon as he said them.

Matt looked at him with blazing eyes. "I don't *let* them do this to me. Look at me. I'm five foot nothing. I weigh nothing. I'm the perfect target for every moron out there. I wet my pants in grade four. Do you think I've ever lived it down?" His voice trailed off into a sob. "Yossi was there. And Yossi packed that little fact in his suitcase and brought it here with him."

"Hey. Sorry. I'm sorry, man. But come on. . . ." Rafe didn't know what to say. He'd never faced this in his entire life.

"And I barfed cutting up a frog in class this year. Yossi's blabbed that nugget, too. That's how it starts."

Rafe made up his mind. "We've got to tell Mr. Longo. He has to know."

"I said no," Matt snapped back. "You, you with your perfect life, you have no clue, do you? If I tell, you know what will happen? You think this was bad? This is nothing. I've had my head shoved in a toilet . . . and held down as they flushed ."

Rafe shook his head. "Mr. Longo will have those

kids tied to a tree for the rest of the week. He could pour honey on them and get a bear and. . . ."

The idea was crazy. They both knew it.

Finally Matt said, "I'll make you a deal. Let me get some sleep. Then tomorrow, in the morning, we'll tell Longo. Okay?"

Rafe hesitated. Then he nodded. "Deal."

Matt went to look for his parka. There was a row of hooks, but no parka in sight. "What a surprise." He swore under his breath.

Rafe took his coat off. "Here. We'll get your coat back. We'll figure this out."

They walked back to cabin five and Rafe put his hand on the knob. *I promised Matt not to tell Longo. But I didn't promise anything else.* He slammed the door open and flicked on the lights.

The boys jumped.

Rafe remembered: be the alpha dog. He yelled. He shook his fist. He twisted his face into something out of a Stephen King horror movie. He kept it going until at last he saw fear in their faces.

"Get back to bed. Not a word. Not a sound. I don't want to hear even a fart. Got it?"

The boys mumbled and lay down on their beds. It was quiet.

Matt glared at Rafe, fury in his eyes.

Rafe turned off the main switch. He crawled into his sleeping bag and was suddenly exhausted. He rolled over and shoved his face into the pillow, begging sleep to come. But no . . . sleep with one eye open, he had been warned. And he didn't like the idea of his back exposed to the jerks in this cabin. So he turned to lay flat and listened to the sounds of the wind. Then he heard the cry of a loon and the howl of a . . . what? A wolf?

It was a lonely sound. An eerie sound. The wolf was calling to others across the vast, ancient forest. In Rafe's mind, he could see the great silver beasts creeping out to hunt.

Rafe felt for the whistle around his neck.

He lay there, wide awake for hours. Then he heard it. Just a creak. A bedspring, that was all. Someone was getting out of bed. Should he say something? What if some kid had to take a leak?

And so he waited. Someone moved across the floor and grabbed a coat off the hook. Then the kid opened the door, slowly, quietly, and slid through the tiniest crack.

Rafe pushed up to his elbow and looked over at the bunks. The bottom bed, Matt's bed, was empty. Rafe listened, straining for any sound. The others hadn't moved. He could hear the heavy, slow breathing of sleep.

Rafe sat all the way up and looked at his watch. Five thirty-three. He'd give Matt ten minutes. That was long enough.

It was a long ten minutes, and at five forty-three,

Matt hadn't come back.

Rafe pulled himself from his sleeping bag and shivered. He slipped on his hiking boots, but didn't bother with the laces. Then he felt for a jacket and was surprised to feel his parka on a hook. Matt must have found his own.

He opened the door and slipped out as quietly as Matt. He stood on the stoop and listened for noises within, but the boys inside didn't move. Then Rafe turned his head and peered into the gray gloom.

Nothing to hear. Nothing to see.

He stepped onto the path and moved carefully toward the bathhouse.

But there was no one there. He checked all the stalls and looked in the towel closet in case Matt was hiding.

Rafe walked the pathway again. In the dim light of pre-dawn he saw the sheen of frost upon the ground. Then he saw them – footprints leading off the path and going down the hill.

Rafe slipped and skidded down the hillside. Then he righted himself by grabbing onto a spruce tree. He saw the footprints again in the clearing. He followed them up another hill. Finally Rafe saw him. The kid was just a small shadow moving against the dull green of the pines.

He hesitated. Should he go back and get someone? But what if he lost Matt's trail? He looked behind him, as if he might see someone rushing to help. And in the next moment, when he swung around, Matt was gone from sight.

Rafe didn't make a real decision. He just took off running.

Chapter 4

Someone Was Screaming

Rafe thought he could overtake Matt in just a few minutes. He'd grab the kid, shake the piss out of him and drag him back to camp. And then . . . then Mr. Longo could deal with him. He was fed up with this kid.

He could see Matt up ahead. He shouted his name but the kid didn't stop. Rafe sprinted across the valley and shouted again. This time Matt spun around, paused for a moment, then took off again.

Rafe swore and charged. He was breathing hard, each breath searing his lungs, but he didn't care. No way a runt like Matt was going to outrun him. They were almost through the clearing and he had to catch him soon. *Go! Faster!* He said the words to himself over and over.

He jumped over a dead log and looked down for a moment to see where his foot would land. Then he watched – like in slow motion – as he stepped on his bootlace and tripped. He rolled hard against a rock.

Rafe scrambled up. His knee was throbbing, his nails filled with dirt.

And Matt was nowhere to be seen in the early morning gloom.

Rafe stood still, willing his heavy breathing to stop, and listened. He could hear thrashing behind him. When he turned toward the sound, he saw branches moving. That way! But as he turned, his knee throbbed. He stopped to grab at his pant leg. No blood, but there'd be quite a bruise.

Don't be a wimp. A bruise is no reason to turn back.

Then he remembered. The whistle. *Stupid! How could he be so stupid?*

Rafe reached inside his jacket and down his sweatshirt to grab the string. He pulled and saw a hunk of broken plastic. The whistle was cracked in half, broken by his fall. Still, Rafe put it to his mouth and blew. The little ball-bearing made a dull rattling noise.

Rafe swore and flung the whistle into the bush. He sat down on the rock and did up his bootlaces.

The smart thing to do was to go back. Matt was his responsibility, but only up to a point. He could go back to the camp and Longo could call for help. Soon police and dogs would track Matt down.

Yup. That was the smart thing to do.

But Rafe didn't like it. It felt like failure. He never failed. Not once. Not in his whole life. No way he was going to start now. Not with . . . . the kid's nickname came into his mind. Not with Doormat.

And not after Longo's warning. Rafe should have been ready.

Rafe stood and surveyed the hill in front of him. Then he spotted some trampled brush and grinned. "Got you now, you little jerk."

Rafe plunged into the trees and into darkness. He pushed branches out of his way, every now and then spotting a freshly broken twig. Here and there, he saw a footprint. He moved as quietly as he could. No calling out Matt's name now. Rafe knew he'd only catch the kid if he surprised him.

Something stung Rafe's neck. Black flies. The flies

swarmed his face and flew into his mouth and nose and eyes. Rafe clutched at his parka, struggling to zip it up as he moved. Then he pulled at the hood and drew the drawstrings tight. He flapped his hands in front of his face and tried to run.

But his boot caught under a root. Rafe sprawled forward, his arms flung out wide as he grabbed for branches. This time he didn't fall. He steadied himself and wiped the sweat from his face. Rafe had to get out of these trees – the sweat was a calling card to the black flies. Another swarm would smell him in no time.

There! Up ahead! Rafe saw a pathway where the earth was smooth. He followed it and could tell the ground was rising steeply upward.

In minutes Rafe was out of the woods and in a small clearing, high on a ridge. In front of him, far across the tree tops, he saw the glimmer of light. Rafe was facing east. Below him was the great tract of forest. But nowhere could he see a sign of Camp Hope.

Lost.

Rafe looked at his watch. *Only half an hour since I left camp and I'm lost.*

He scratched at the bites on his face.

He kept looking for the camp. There should be

smoke from a breakfast fire. There should be light from the cookhouse.

But all Rafe could see was the small shadow of a person. It was Matt, standing in a small bit of scrub. The kid, too, was staring into the sky where the sun would rise.

Rafe smiled and moved silently. Matt shouldn't have let his guard down. In seconds he was close . . . so close. . . .

Rafe flew at the kid from behind and tackled him at the knees.

Matt folded in a heap. Then he twisted about to grab hold, shoving his fingers into Rafe's face.

Rafe jerked back and managed to climb part way up, but then he winced as he put pressure on his bruised knee.

In that second of weakness, Matt shoved him, knocking Rafe to the side.

Now fury fuelled Rafe and he leaped to his feet, fist raised. He was ready to punch the life out of this stupid moron.

But Rafe didn't get a chance. Instead, his boot skidded on the loose stones. His feet slipped out from under him. Rafe was over the side of the cliff before he knew what had happened.

He saw Matt's face above him – terrified. The kid was shouting something, but Rafe couldn't hear the words.

Rafe hit a rock, then another, then a third. He clutched wildly at shrubs and roots. Someone was screaming. The roaring in his head was like a jet engine.

Then something caught at him, grabbing him, holding him.

In that moment of stillness, Rafe knew the screams weren't from someone else. The screams were his.

He heard the snap of branches and he fell again. This time he landed hard on his head.

Another sound slammed into his skull, and then blackness flooded his brain.

Chapter 5

A Real Nightmare

Nightmare!

The nightmare went on and on. The moose stood on the highway, unmoving, until the car rammed into it. Diana was by his side, gorgeous in her prom dress. She was screaming at him. Blood pouring from her head.

No! He swerved. They were both in a ditch, and the moose charged off into the bush. But now Matt was in the car, shouting, "Told you. Tomorrow we die."

Then Rafe was falling. He grabbed onto Matt and the two flew out into space.

The ground was coming up fast and he pulled at the rip cord. But it was only a plastic whistle, broken in half. Then Matt let go of him and laughed. "Told you. Tomorrow we die."

Rafe was being pulled, pulled apart, and the pain was terrible.

The crack. The sound of that crack would never leave him. Because. . . .

Because he wasn't dead. He was alive.

Rafe tried to open his eyes, but his left eyelid seemed glued shut. He rubbed at it with his hand, and his fingers came away covered in blood. He squinted through his right eye and saw he was lying on flat ground under trees. It was dark, and he shivered.

Matt was watching him.

"I didn't mean this. I didn't mean for you to fall," he said.

Rafe turned his head to one side and felt the throbbing. He tried to speak but no sound came out. He swallowed and licked dry lips and muttered, "What happened?"

"You slipped. I didn't push you. I didn't. Then you landed in tree branches. I tried to get to you. I did. I got down the cliff and then I saw you fall to the ground."

Rafe nodded. Tree branches. He remembered them on the way down. That's what held him. Saved

his life.

"Then I dragged you here. We were only a little way from these trees. So I dragged you here and waited with you. I didn't leave you."

Rafe caught the tone in Matt's voice. The defensive "don't blame me" tone. Again he wondered what was going on with this kid.

Rafe swallowed again and tasted the sourness of his mouth. He suddenly realized he'd been lying here a long time. He tried to sit up but was quickly dizzy. When he lay back down he winced as his head met ground.

But Rafe could move his feet and legs and arms and felt a rush of gratitude. Somehow . . . some way, he had survived the fall. Nothing seemed broken.

He brought his arm up to his good eye and looked at his watch. Smashed. "You have a watch? What time is it?"

"Six."

Only six? Then why did Rafe think so much time had passed? "We have to get out from under these trees," he said. "They have to be able to see us when they start looking. I can't get back to camp on my own. And I don't even know where camp is. We're lost."

Matt glanced away. "They've been looking for us," he replied. "All day yesterday. It's Monday morning."

Rafe forced himself to sit up, biting back the nausea. "Twenty-four hours? We've been here a full day?"

Matt nodded. "I couldn't just leave you out there, so I pulled you under the trees. Then I saw a helicopter fly over and so . . . so I stayed."

Rafe couldn't follow this. "You saw them and hid?

Why didn't you wave or something?"

Matt didn't say anything.

Something added up in Rafe's mind and he said, "You didn't want the helicopter to find you. You don't want to go back."

"You've finally figured that out?" Matt asked. "Look – I only came up here to Camp Hope to run away. I don't want to *survive* any longer. Know what I was thinking on the bus when we saw the accident? I thought, why wasn't it me in that car? A few seconds and it's over."

Matt said it quietly. No anger, no bitterness, no smart-ass kid being defiant. Rafe knew he meant it. But something ugly in him made him say, "You could off yourself in the city."

"I could. But it's harder. Too many nosy social workers around. Getting lost in the woods and slowly going out seemed better. Cleaner, somehow. Like disappearing into the earth."

"If you hadn't seen the chopper, you were going to leave me." Rafe made it a statement, not a question.

"Look. It wasn't supposed to happen like this. You were asleep. You weren't supposed to follow me." He shrugged. "And I didn't leave you. I waited until you came to."

Rafe put a hand to the back of his head and felt where blood had crusted around a huge bump. His fingers traced the slit of a cut and he could tell it needed stitches. Too late, now. He knew that. Stitches had to be done within a couple of hours or else. Now he had to hope the cut wasn't infected because. . . . He wanted to live. He had escaped death and he wasn't going to die now, no matter what Matt wanted to do.

But he was so cold.

"They'll come back, you know," Rafe said. "They won't stop looking for us."

"I left a letter in my duffle bag. I said I was hitching back to the city. I said I hated this place. By now they've found it and are looking for me everywhere but here."

Rafe was impressed. "Clever. But what about me? Don't you think they'll look for me?"

Matt had an answer. "They'll figure you chased after me. Maybe they'll think you ran back to the city, too. Maybe they'll think we got picked up by a serial killer. Whatever. But they'll follow the trail the other way."

Rafe pounced. "But when we don't show up in the city, they'll know. They'll intensify the search around the camp." He felt like he had scored a huge point with this moron.

But Matt slowly shook his head. "What? Another two, three days? Know where I'll be by then? Long gone. Lost." He laughed. "But hey! Cheer up. I hope they find you."

Rafe knew he was beat. The kid had it all figured out. "So you're not staying with me? You're leaving?"

Matt glared at him. "I'm not a killer. I took care of you. But now, now you're awake and alive and you can do whatever you want." He turned away.

He looked so small and so lonely that Rafe said, "Why? Why do you want to. . ." He didn't finish that question. "Why don't you want to live?"

"Nobody cares about me. No one ever has. I get picked on all the time. I have no future, no nothing."

"But you're only fourteen. You can turn it around. You've got time."

"That's not a message losers like me can hear."

Rafe started to argue but then pain cut into his gut and he was suddenly starving. Right on cue his stomach rumbled. "So I guess if you're planning on dying you didn't bring any food with you?"

"Eat bark."

Rafe wanted to punch him, but knew he didn't have the strength. Instead he felt around his coat and found a half pack of gum in the inner pocket. He offered a stick to Matt. "Want one? Or is gum not part of your death rite?"

Matt grabbed at it and soon the smell of Juicy Fruit filled the air. But then, the saliva made the hunger pangs worse and Rafe's head began to pound. He wanted to lie down and sleep but he knew not to. With a head injury, that was the worst thing. He was lucky he wasn't off in a la-la land coma right now.

Water. He had to find water. Rafe knew he could survive a few weeks without food, but only three days without water. He pushed himself up to his knees and crawled until he was in the open.

He saw now that Matt had dragged him under a large pine. Its lower branches hung down and swept the ground forming a natural tent. All about him were other large trees and the upper branches blocked the sky. Rafe stood slowly and moved unsteadily, watching where he stepped, pausing to look up, until at last there was a gap in the trees, and he could see dark gray clouds.

A little farther and Rafe was in a small clearing.

Perfect! This is where he could wait. Because he knew that if you got lost in the woods, it was best to stay put. If you tried to find your way out, you'd probably go in circles or get deeper into the forest. He'd sit here and watch for a helicopter and find a way to attract attention.

How long could it take? Not long, Rafe felt sure. He'd be fine if he didn't panic.

But then, the first few snowflakes began to fall.

Chapter 6

Storm

Within seconds the temperature dropped and the wind picked up. Rafe could see a squall blowing in. He heard a noise and saw Matt stepping over the rocks.

"We have to have shelter or we'll freeze to death," Rafe shouted. He pulled up his hood. "Holing up under a tree won't be enough."

Matt smiled. "Good luck, Rafe. Hope you make it."

Matt was close enough for Rafe to reach out and grab him. "What the . . . ?! Are you serious? Do you . . . ."

But Matt did . . . want to die, that is. Rafe let go, and Matt backed away from him. Rafe watched the kid until he was out of the clearing and hidden by brush.

"I don't care," Rafe yelled. "Go – yourself! I'm not your keeper!"

Could he do this? Let the kid go?

Fatigue washed over him. *Got to think.* He couldn't help Matt. You can't help someone who doesn't want to be helped. Now he had to save himself.

The truth of it hit like a ton of bricks. Rafe felt a scream rising up inside him. But instead, the only noise he made was a bitten-off sob. *Can't do this. Can't break down out here!*

As long as it snowed, no one would be able to look for him. He had to survive until. . . .

He sat on a rock and tried to think about survival. He'd studied this in school. He should be able to remember that much. Then Rafe remembered: STOP. Stop. Think. Observe. Plan.

He was stopped all right. Now think.

Rule number one: don't get lost. Well, so much for that. Rule number two: keep warm. Rafe glanced about and saw branches on the ground. He gathered as many as he could and dragged them over to the tree tent. Then he hurried back for more.

Rafe shoved them into a flattened pile. Then he

found dead leaves and scraps of bark to stuff in the cracks. Not much of a bed, but at least he'd be off the ground. Otherwise, the cold earth would steal his body heat.

Back in the open, he looked for low hanging branches with pine needles. Then he hacked at them with a rock until they snapped. He shook the bit of snow off and laid them on top of his bed. A blanket. Not much of a blanket, but something. Then Rafe collected a handful more. He tried to weave them in and out of the bottom branches of the tree. It might make some sort of roof.

The storm was gathering force. Rafe ran to a drift of snow and scooped up handfuls of snow, stuffing them into his mouth. At least he now had water.

For a moment there was the relief of something wet in his mouth. Only a moment. But then the pain hit his throat and knifed into his chest. His stomach reacted fast, and he doubled over with cramps.

He forced himself to breathe deeply and slowly. In a minute or so, he was able to stand up. Never eat snow, that's another rule. He had forgotten that one.

Rafe picked up a handful of snow and rubbed it over his face, shivering at the cold. He held a bit on his left eye and then moved it around gently. At last the crusted blood came loose and he could open his eye.

But he still had to have water. *Think!*

Rafe tugged at the ripped pocket on his jacket until it was off. He stuffed it with snow and then crawled under the tree. He wrapped the pocket in dead leaves and held it in his hands until the snow began to melt. He noticed for the first time how scratched his hands were. Three fingernails were broken deep in the nail bed and several bruises were darkening along his swollen knuckles.

Ignore it! He blew on the pocket of snow as if he were polishing glass. When he had a small puddle of water, he sipped it slowly. This time he let each bit of liquid move around his mouth. When it was warm enough, he let the water slide down his throat. He kept doing this, over and over, until his makeshift cup was empty.

Rafe went back out into the open again. By now the snow was coming down so thickly he could barely see in front of him. Rafe grabbed at the snow and rolled it into loose snowballs, making as many as he could, until his hands were aching and red and numb. He kicked the snowballs under the branches with his feet.

Then, pleased with his work, he crawled back in.

He huddled on top of his bed, knees tucked tight to his chest. Rafe leaned against the tree and tugged the pine branches up about him. Then he thought to pull his arms out of the sleeves of his parka. He cupped his hands in his armpits. Then he slid his chin under the collar.

I'm like a turtle, he thought.

Rafe might have smiled at the idea. But not here. Not now.

Chapter 7

Survival

Rafe heard the sudden roar of wind as it smashed into the tree tops. Icy pellets found every chink above him. They rained down like bullets.

He hunched himself into a small ball, pushing farther into his nest. He turned his head toward the trunk of the tree. Then he squeezed his eyes shut.

Rafe's thoughts raced in all directions. But they all ended the same way.

Death.

There was a loud crack over his head. Rafe strained to see into the gloom. A tree crashed down toward him, and he rolled – only a bit, but it was enough. The falling pine caught in the fork of a branch. It held just a few feet above him.

Rafe looked to his side. A dead branch was driven into the ground like a spear. That's where he had been just a second before.

The pounding of his blood drowned out the wailing of the storm. And yet, over all that, he could hear whimpering. There were little sobbing noises like a kitten mewling.

With a shock Rafe realized the sobbing came from him.

Rafe clamped his lips shut.

He willed himself to take deep breaths to calm down. He counted to five with each breath in and out. At last his heart slowed and the pounding of his blood stopped. Rafe was in total darkness now – with the downed tree, there was no light at all.

Then Rafe noticed something strange – the sleet wasn't coming down on him. The fallen tree gave him more protection.

Strangely, he felt safe here. He felt protected by the branches and the darkness.

Rafe fumbled around, hunting for a snowball. Then he went through the ritual of melting and sipping it slowly.

If he could survive the storm. . . . If he could make his way out to the clearing. . . . If he could hold on until someone found him. . . .

If, if, if.

But he was so hungry.

Rafe knew he had to stay awake. Falling asleep outside was certain death. But he suddenly felt very warm. His shelter seemed very, very cozy. Rafe pulled himself into a little ball again and thought he was like a field mouse, holed up for winter.

His eyelids drooped. Rafe remembered books he had read as a child about bunnies and squirrels. In his mind, he was in his mother's lap. She was reading to him, tucking him into bed.

His mother was singing a lullaby. Rafe closed his eyes and slept and dreamed he was floating in space. He felt unhooked from his body, weightless and free.

Then the dream turned against him. Something was pushing him. Something was clawing at him, struggling to tear him apart. Monsters shouted at him, threatening death. Something was sitting on him so he couldn't breathe. He heard a voice calling.

"Wake up, Rafe. Your time isn't up yet. Wake up, my dear." It was his grandmother.

But his grandmother was dead. His grandmother was already dead.

Rafe heard a mangled, garbled sound. It was the half-swallowed scream of someone in a nightmare. Then he was fully awake, shaking and shivering. His own horrible cry echoed in his head.

Rafe couldn't stop his teeth from chattering. He pushed his arms back into his sleeves and brought his hands up to his face. He blew softly into his hands, holding them over his mouth.

Then he listened. The forest was quiet. The wind had stopped. Maybe the storm was over. But for some reason, the silence filled Rafe with more dread than before. He didn't want to die like this, hidden in a burrow like an animal. He didn't want his body discovered by hikers, years from now, his bones picked clean.

He thought of Matt. Was that the death he wanted? Just to . . . what did he say? Just to disappear into the earth. He wondered if Matt's wish was coming true.

Move! said a voice. It came from inside him. Rafe didn't know what time it was or how long he had been sleeping, but he knew he had to move.

He untucked his legs and stretched. The nerves

tingled up and down. Rafe yelped in pain, but he forced himself to move. He rolled to his knees and tried to push apart the branches. He saw they were frozen together with ice.

His shelter had become a prison. That which had saved him now locked him in.

Rafe clawed at the branches. As they shook loose, snow and chunks of ice fell about him. He rolled onto his back and tried to kick with his feet, but . . . his feet were numb.

"No, no, no, no," he whimpered. Rafe struggled to undo the laces, to pull off his boots. But the laces were knotted with ice.

Rafe scrubbed at his left boot with his elbow. At last he could pick at the knots and pull off the boot. He cradled his foot in his lap and rubbed his toes until he felt the nerves stabbing. This time he smiled at the pain. No frostbite. Not yet.

Rafe slid the boot back on, flexing his foot, wiggling his toes as he did so. Then he repeated the whole thing with his right foot.

But this time . . . no tingling. He rubbed harder and hit the sole of his foot with his fist. Nothing.

Rafe suddenly saw himself in the hospital, his foot cut off. Diana would be there holding his hand, crying. But he'd never able to ski or play football or skate or. . . .

Stop! Don't go there. Don't! Rafe knew he'd never survive if he gave in to despair.

He kicked at the branches near the ground with his left foot. At last he heard a cracking sound. Above him was a glimmer of light. Rafe rolled on his side and shoved at the ice and snow. Soon he had an opening big enough to crawl through.

Outside, the sky was dark and heavy with clouds. There was no way to figure out what time it was. Was it still today? Or was it tomorrow? Rafe felt as if he had lurched into a frozen time warp.

Knock it off! Smarten up! It could snow again any moment, but for now, there was time. Rafe sat up and looked behind him. His tent was a frozen igloo. Ice coated the long branches, keeping out the storm.

There was irony here, Rafe thought. *Must tell my English teacher next week.*

Laughter bubbled up from somewhere inside him. Soon Rafe was laughing like an idiot. He laughed so hard that tears poured from his eyes. *Oh, this can't be good,* he thought. But Rafe couldn't stop. He wiped at his face but there was something so wildly stupid about all this. How could he, Rafe Reynolds, end up dying all alone in the wilderness? How could it happen? Just because he wanted to give something back. Well, he was giving something back, all right. His entire life.

But not yet. He wasn't giving up just yet. The storm was over and he had a chance.

The wind had blown the snow up against hills and rock. The ground wasn't clear, but the snow was no longer heavy. This meant he could forge a path. Rafe found a branch on the ground and using it as a cane, stood up. He felt nothing in his right foot, but at least he didn't feel pain.

Then, suddenly, he was light-headed. Dots appeared in front of him. If not for the cane, he would have fallen.

In front of him, a path into the trees led downhill. That was a good sign. More likely a road would be at the bottom of a hill than at the top. Rafe decided to make a start and see how far he got. If it began to snow right away, he could follow his footprints back and find his shelter again.

Then he remembered something from his training. The signal for distress is a triangle. If someone flew overhead and saw a triangle on the ground, they would know he was close by.

Rafe found three sturdy branches and lay them in the design. They were bulky enough not to get covered with snow. Or so he hoped. Rafe looked at his triangle and felt pleased with himself. Then he shook his head.

I'm out of my mind!

He began walking downhill.

It was slow going. Rafe watched for patches of ice and hidden tree roots. He stopped to rest every few minutes and whenever he did, he held his breath and listened.

He didn't expect to hear a plane. Not really, not in this weather.

But he didn't expect to hear the low snarling either.

Chapter 8

Bobcat and Bears

The animal dropped down from the branches above. It landed on Rafe's back, slashing with bared claws at his head.

Rafe screamed and fell to the ground. He turned and twisted, pushing at the soft, wet fur. He felt the sting as a claw raked over his knuckles. Then another.

Rafe groped about blindly for his walking stick. When his hand closed over it, he brought the stick up and swung. Rafe felt the jolt as the stick made contact.

The animal was a small blur of gray and white. It snarled when Rafe hit it. So Rafe hit it again, and once more.

Then, without notice, it was gone.

Rafe lay there, stunned. It must have been a bobcat. Or a lynx. But they didn't attack humans, unless. . . . Unless they were starving.

Rafe felt the icy tingle of fear in his gut. It was early spring, and there had been a storm. And the animals were desperate for food.

Food, any kind of food. Living or dead.

Rafe stumbled to his feet. He had to get down this hill. One foot, then the other. One foot, then the other. Again and again. Over and over. One foot, then the other.

He came out from under the trees into a clearing the size of a front lawn.

And then he saw the trail of blood.

For a moment, Rafe was confused. He thought it was blood from the bobcat. Had he hurt it? No, not enough to draw blood. So then, this had to mean. . . . Another animal?

He knew he had to get away, fast. If he came across a wounded animal. . . .

Game over.

He moved carefully, pausing with each step to listen.

He had passed through the clearing and was almost

at the edge of the forest when he saw the heap of clothing. And more blood.

In front of him was Matt. But this Matt wasn't moving. It was just Matt's body.

Rafe froze. He suddenly felt as if something was watching him. He strained to see out the corners of his eyes and then slowly forced himself to turn his head and look about.

Nothing. Or . . . nothing that he could see.

He stumbled forward and onto his knees beside the boy. He saw the ugly slash marks across Matt's forehead and again on his right hand. And he saw the blood seeping through the coat.

"Matt?" he whispered. He put his face down beside the boy and listened for breath. He slid his fingers in under the collar to feel for a pulse.

He couldn't hear anything, but he could feel a faint beat. "Matt," he said louder. "Come on, Matt. Wake up. It's Rafe. Come on, buddy."

Rafe loosened Matt's fingers and looked at the jacket. The front was ripped and underneath. . . . Through the shreds of his sweatshirt, Rafe saw the same wicked slashes on Matt's chest.

Bile filled Rafe's mouth. He turned and retched, over and over. The pain of it scorched his throat as he vomited nothing. Rafe was hot and dizzy. Sweat beaded on his forehead and neck. Rafe reached for snow and swabbed his face. He stuffed snow into his mouth and spit it out, again and again. When he could steady his breathing, he turned back to the young boy on the ground.

Now Matt's eyes were open, staring.

But he wasn't looking at Rafe. He was looking

behind him, and he was scared.

Rafe forced himself to turn around. Then he saw what Matt saw.

The bear – ten metres away.

Rafe couldn't move. His mind went blank.

The huge, massive head of the bear swung slowly side to side. It had its nose in the air, trying to catch a scent.

Rafe stared at the great hulk of black fur and held his breath. And then, his thoughts suddenly came into focus.

It was a black bear. It was spring.

Cubs.

A black bear. Not a grizzly. You could escape a black bear by making noise. Scaring it. Then backing away, slowly.

One chance. I have one chance. He felt about on the ground for the walking stick, never taking his eyes off the bear.

The bear lowered its head, then took a step toward him, unsteady on its feet. It was still groggy with deep winter sleep.

Rafe inched his way to standing. He tensed his muscles, threw the stick into the woods to his left.

It smacked into a tree with a loud crack, then landed with a heavy thud.

For a moment, the bear didn't react. But slowly it turned its head to follow the noise.

To Rafe, it felt like forever. But finally, slowly, the bear swung round. In a few seconds it had shuffled into the woods.

"Rafe," he heard. It was no louder than a child's whisper.

Rafe went over to Matt, and he forced himself to smile. "We have to get away," he said. "How bad . . . I mean. . . ." His voice trailed off.

"I don't know . . . I'm not sure. . . . Fainted." Matt winced and lay still on the ground.

"The bear did this?" Stupid question.

Matt nodded. "I had to find shelter. In a hillside. Cave or . . . or something. Then I saw them. Two of them. Babies."

"And she came back? The mother bear?"

"She swiped at me but I ran. She went to the cubs and I escaped."

Rafe took a deep breath. "We have to get away from here. She won't . . . I mean, I don't think she'll follow us. She'll stay with her cubs. But we can't sit here waiting. When we're a ways off, I'll take a look at . . . at what she did. Can you stand?"

Rafe waited for an answer and then realized Matt had passed out.

And it was getting dark. Another day was almost over.

Have to find shelter. Have to. Rafe knew he couldn't get back to his fort, not all that way back uphill, not with Matt to worry about. But. . . .

Why worry about Matt? Why not leave him here? He wanted to die. He just about got his wish. No one would blame you. If you get out alive, that is. Screw him. This is all his fault. Leave the fool and save yourself.

Rafe took a step backward. He had two options. Alone, without Matt, he could get up to his fort and known shelter. Then, in the morning, start down the hill again. Or, without Matt, he didn't have to go back. He could keep going. He could find shelter for himself somehow. So . . . two options. Without Matt.

And if Matt died?

Don't be stupid! Gotta look out for yourself. What about your mom and dad? You want them to deal with your death?

He took another step, then another. The voice kept

hammering away in his head.

And what about Diana? You want to never see her again? Plenty of guys around ready to step into your shoes.

The image of Diana flooded his thoughts and poured warmth into his body. He saw her smile and he heard her laugh. Almost, almost, he saw her watching him now, her head tilted to one side. "Rafe? What is it, babe?"

The blackness in his mind lifted.

And with that, Rafe shook his head, embarrassed by his own ugly, dark thoughts. *How did I come to this? Live and let die?*

He looked at Matt and something slunk back into his mind. *Shelter. Matt said "I found shelter." You don't look for shelter if you want to die. So. . . .*

Something had happened to Matt. Maybe he didn't want to die anymore. And he ran from the bear. He said he "escaped."

Anger pushed up inside and Rafe shook Matt. "Wake up! Come on, Matt! Wake up!" He grabbed a fistful of snow and wiped it over the boy's white face.

Matt didn't stir and Rafe stared at his body, all five feet nothing of it.

Rafe went back to get the stick he'd thrown into the

woods. Then he got down on his knees and, pushing and pulling and dragging, he managed to hoist Matt up onto his back. He leaned on his cane and thrust himself to his feet. *Probably better that Matt is out cold.*

One step, then another, out of the clearing, into the woods. One step, then another. . . . Matt wasn't heavy, but Rafe was so tired and his right foot was useless. And he had to have water soon.

In the gathering twilight, Rafe banged his shin up against a fallen tree. A huge one. He walked the length of it, back to where its enormous ball of roots splayed up against a hillside of rock. The mass of roots made a roof of sorts.

It would have to do.

He lowered Matt and dragged him in between the tree and the rock. He got out his pocket cup and gathered snow. The he sat down beside Matt to go through the business of preparing water.

For a moment, he stared at the gash on his hand not remembering. Bobcat.

He shuddered and peered into the trees above him.

Then he heard a sound – the eerie, lonely howling of a wolf.

Except the wolf wasn't alone. Rafe heard three

answering calls.

And the scent of blood – Rafe's and Matt's – was in the air.

Chapter 9

Alive

Rafe slept fitfully, dozing and waking and dozing again. Sometimes he sat up with a jerk, only to slide back to sleep moments later.

In the morning, he was confused. He didn't know if the orange, glowing eyes that watched him through the night were in his dreams or real. He shivered and felt that he would never get warm again. The damp was deep in his bones.

Damp. That meant the weather had changed. The air was warmer and so the threat of more snow was gone – for now.

Rafe moved his cramped legs and arms and rolled away from Matt. He had slept the night curled beside the boy. He hoped their double body heat might help them stay warm.

"Matt?" Rafe's voice was hoarse and his mouth was dry. When Matt didn't answer, Rafe checked to see if he was still breathing. Yes, still alive. So Rafe crawled out from the roots.

The sky was still overcast and gray, but snow was melting and dripping off branches and down the rock face. Rafe pushed his face against the stone and licked all that he could. Then he filled the pocket cup and went back to Matt. Propping the kid up, he held the scooped square of canvas to his lips.

In a few moments, Matt opened his eyes.

Rafe helped him sip more water. Then he told Matt what had happened.

"You carried me?" Matt's voice was raspy.

Rafe shrugged. "No big deal. You're a runt."

Matt's eyes were clouded, but still he mumbled, "Thanks."

Rafe cleared his throat and looked away. "So now," he said, "we have to have a plan. I don't want to spend another night out here, but I'm worried we'll walk around in circles. Maybe we have to stay still so search planes can find us. That means we have to find the

right spot."

Matt struggled to sit up. He gasped and grabbed at his chest.

"Easy, easy. I've got to take a look, Matt. Okay?" Rafe didn't wait for an answer. He grappled with the zipper and opened Matt's coat. Then he lifted the sweatshirt and stared.

The bear had swiped hard at Matt's chest. Three claws had made contact and the welts were red-raw.

That was good, wasn't it? At least the bleeding had stopped,
Rafe thought. He covered the wound again and then
looked at Matt's scalp. There were four deep cuts.
Chunks of hair and skin were missing.

Rafe willed himself not to be sick.

"Well," he finally said, "I can safely say that you
and I both need medical attention." And he smiled
when he saw that Matt tried to laugh.

"Come on. Let's get going." Rafe half dragged Matt
out into the open. He cracked off another support
stick from the old roots and handed it to Matt. "Can
you walk at all?"

Matt managed to stand, hunched over the stick.
Rafe put his arm around him, and they moved ahead.
Slowly, they got around the dead tree and back to the
path.

"Let me know if you're tired. We can rest. And I
can carry you some more."

"Where . . . where are we going?" Matt asked.

Rafe wanted to scream "how the – should I know?"
but he said, "Just downhill. I figure we have a better
chance of being seen in the valley." He thought of
something else. "You know, we can't be that far away
from the camp. There's no way we wandered miles

and miles. They have to find us soon."

The idea encouraged them both. Rafe moved a bit faster, pulling on Matt's arm. But the boy had to stop every few steps and take deep breaths. Once, Matt put his hand to his head and winced. Rafe thought for sure the kid was going to pass out again.

They were under the trees when the rain started. At first, Rafe thought it was melting snow, but no. He heard the steady *plunk, plunk, plunk* as raindrops hit the ground. When they reached another small clearing, the rain was coming down hard.

"If we wait it out, we'll get drenched. And who knows how long it'll last. We have to keep going," he told Matt.

Matt nodded, but Rafe saw there was no strength in it. *Kid's dead if we don't get help,* he thought. Rafe tightened his arm around Matt and plodded on. He was soaked in minutes. Matt didn't seem to notice.

Suddenly, Rafe's foot slid into a rut and they smashed to the ground. Matt rolled away and lay there, not making a sound. Rafe swore and pulled himself up. He could already feel the throbbing in his left ankle.

Rafe leaned against a tree until the pain dropped.

Then he hoisted Matt onto his back and limped forward.

Hold on. Hold on. Keep going. Hold on. One step. One more step. One more step. Again. Hold on.

He'd read about stories like this. About survivors. He'd seen movies about people surviving against all odds. People in war. His grandfather had been in World War II. Caught behind enemy lines. Put in a prison camp. Marching. Starving. Marching again. Young men. Teenagers his age.

I can do this.

Rafe stopped and looked up at the leaden sky. "I can do this!" he shouted, and he listened to his voice echo in the stillness. He wondered if his grandfather could hear him. He wondered if anybody could hear him.

He turned around in a slow circle and saw it – the small hut across the clearing.

His heart pounded against his rib cage as if it would explode. He began to run toward the hut, limping and staggering like he was drunk.

"Matt! Look! Look!"

There was hardly any snow on this flat bit of ground. So Rafe began running faster.

Halfway there, Rafe felt his foot slip out sideways. He staggered, losing his grip on Matt. Then he kept going, sliding, tumbling, until he felt something crumble beneath him.

The shock of the sudden cold water hit him like a punch. He couldn't breathe. When he gasped for air, ice water rushed into his mouth. He kicked wildly and flung out his arms and smacked into something hard – a submerged log. He grappled and held on.

But his body was so heavy . . . and his boots dragged him down . . . and his mind told him to let go and sleep.

One hand slipped off the log. He tried to imagine himself swimming to the surface, but it was so cold and he was so tired. Somehow he saw his family and Diana off on the solid ground. He called out to them but they didn't answer. They didn't smile or wave. They watched him struggle.

He heard a voice in his head. *We can't help you now, Rafe. You have to do it for yourself.*

But I'm so tired. I need to sleep. I'll sleep for just a bit, then I'll try again.

Then something grabbed at his head and yanked.

Rafe's face cleared the water and he took a breath

of air. The air stung like salt on a cut and burned into his lungs.

There was a voice. It was Matt, screaming at him. "Rafe! Kick! Come on! You can do it! I've got you, just kick! Kick!"

Over on the shore his family watched. *You have to help yourself. We can't save you.*

Matt stretched out his other hand. "Grab on! Rafe! Grab onto me!"

Rafe smiled. "Just a little nap," he mumbled.

Matt screamed again and pulled. Rafe felt himself inching up out of the water.

He wondered at the look on Matt's face. He looked so . . . so strong.

Something clicked in Rafe's brain and he tried to pull his arm out of the water. But his arm was so heavy and his muscles didn't work. He couldn't tell his arm to lift up.

"Again, Rafe! Come on!"

Rafe knew he had to pull his arm out of the water just so he could wave to his family. He knew they were still there.

"Rafe!"

He tried once more. He watched his arm move

through the water, like it wasn't his own arm, just something floating in the water.

But it is my arm. And I have to move it. No one else can move my arm.

Somehow he managed to pull it out of the water. And he looked at it – his arm – as if he had never seen it before.

Then other arms were around him, yanking, until Rafe was half out of the water.

And then Rafe knew to dig his elbows into the frozen surface and drag his body forward. He managed a mighty kick and hauled his legs out of the lake.

Rafe glanced over at the shore behind him. His family was gone.

He felt Matt grab his wrists and pull him across the snow. In no time, they were at the door of the hut.

His last thought was one word.

Chapter 10

Last Chance

Rafe opened his eyes. He was on a bed, naked, and the blankets covering him smelled of dust. He saw rough wooden walls. From the corner, Matt was watching him.

"Welcome back," Matt said.

With a sense of repeating himself, Rafe asked, "How long?"

Matt shrugged. "It's daytime. And it isn't snowing. Maybe they'll look. . . ." He took a long, breath. "Look for us today."

Rafe waited a moment before answering. He noticed how pale Matt was, and he saw that the scabs on his head were bleeding again. "You want somebody to find you. Why?"

Matt looked away. Rafe closed his eyes. He had almost dozed off when the kid finally spoke.

"When the storm started, I looked for shelter," Matt said. "When the bear attacked me, I ran."

Minutes ticked by. Rafe waited.

Matt cleared his throat. "And then I knew . . . I *knew* I never really wanted to die. Pretty lame, eh? It *is* my life and I want to hang on to it. It didn't matter what anyone else did to me or thought of me." Another long pause. "I felt. . . ." Matt frowned, trying to find the right word. "Anger," he finally said. "All that . . . all that stuff I said before. That was just trash . . . talk. . . ." His voice trailed off.

Rafe remembered his crazy dream out on the water – his family saying he had to save himself. And he understood what had happened to Matt. It made sense. "You have to want to live," Rafe told him. "No one can give you that."

Matt coughed and held his chest. "Yeah, well. How do we do that? Get out of this mess, I mean?"

Rafe pushed himself up and looked about him.

The hut was the size of a large closet. Aside from the iron bed, there was no other furniture. There was a calendar on the wall – 1958. The calendar had a cheesy picture of a woman in a bathing suit leaning over a car. There was a lantern on a hook above his clothes, a beaten up Coleman. That was it.

Watching Rafe's eyes, Matt said, "There's a bit of kerosene in the lamp. And I found this." He held up a notebook chewed by mice. "It looks like this was a cabin for some forestry guy."

Rafe lay back down. "Judging by the calendar, I guess it hasn't been used for a while. No one's coming here soon to save us." Then he remembered something. "You stripped me?"

Matt nodded. "Had to. You were soaked and saying crazy things. I didn't want you to die."

Rafe heaved himself up and rolled off the bed, holding tight to the blankets. He put his feet on the floor and fell. In panic he looked at his feet. His toes were white. All of them.

Don't think about it. Don't!

Rafe crawled to his clothes, frozen and stiff. Then he lay his head down on the rough wood and felt the sting of tears.

Only then did he see it. The match. One wooden match. It had fallen between the floorboards.

Rafe grappled for it like a crazy man. He tried to shove his thick, frozen fingers into the crack. No way he could reach the match.

Matt just stared at him, as if he'd gone crazy.

Rafe looked about and grabbed the drawstring of the hood on his parka. He pushed the plastic tip of it into the crack. Then slowly, oh so slowly, he poked until one end of the match raised up. At last he could pry it out.

He held the match in the air. "It might be our lucky day, Matt."

Then he picked up the Coleman lantern and shook it gently. Matt was right. A dribble of kerosene splashed inside it.

Matt was lying down now. "Maybe we can have some heat until they find us," he said.

But Rafe shook his head. "No. Not enough kerosene for that. We don't know when . . . if . . . they'll find us. We have to be smart."

"So let's light a fire. A big one," Matt answered. He stood up and stumbled to the door, leaning on the wall for support.

Rafe saw the effort this took. He saw Matt's face go white as a ghost.

Matt pushed open the door, half falling outside. There was no rain or snow or wind. And the sun shone.

"What if we. . . ." Matt sank down to his knees in the slush. "What if . . . use blankets . . . fire?"

Rafe understood. "Burn the hut?"

Matt nodded.

"But if. . . ." Rafe knew if they burned the hut and no one saw it . . . that was it. *Their last chance.*

Rafe's thoughts darted every which way. Was anyone still looking for them? Where were they? Would anyone see the smoke? And what then? What if it didn't work? But in the end, the choice came from his gut. *Matt was right.*

The hut was old wood. *It should go up pretty quick.*

Rafe pulled the mattress off the bed onto the floor. He lay the lantern in the middle. Then he tucked the most rotten blanket around it, keeping the other for himself.

"Use the calendar," Matt said. He was leaning on the door frame, too weak to help.

Rafe nodded. He ripped up the old calendar, using

the paper as tinder.

It was time, Rafe knew. *One match, that's all we've got.*

Rafe's hand shook as he scraped the match down the rough side of the iron bed frame. Three tries and nothing. Soon the sulfur would be gone from the head. And that would be it. Done. Finished. They'd be waiting to die.

But the fourth time the flame spurted. Rafe held it to the lantern wick and prayed. One tiny flame. One small match.

They smelled it first – the smell of kerosene – before they saw the flame.

"Now! Do it now!" Matt cried.

Rafe nodded and tipped the lantern on its side. They both watched until the burning kerosene found the ripped paper and old cloth. Quickly the fire spread across the floor.

Rafe scrambled backward, crablike, to Matt. Then they dragged themselves away from the hut to wait. Rafe was suddenly overwhelmed with fatigue, hunger and pain.

If we're wrong. . . . If we've blown this chance. . . .

It was an eternity before the flames spread. But

then the fire grew quickly. The flames licked up the walls and caught the rotted roof. Soon the whole cabin was on fire, sending a beacon of smoke into the sky.

Chapter 11

"Tell Me!"

The plane flew over, then turned and veered away.

It seemed as if hours passed as they huddled together by the lake. They kept drifting in and out of awareness. Neither of them knew what was real and what was nightmare.

Slowly the cabin fire spread to some nearby trees. Then animals came out of the forest. They headed toward the lake for safety. One moose came forward through the slushy ice and stopped close by. Rafe stared into its eyes and measured the width of its antlers. Then Matt held out his arm as if to pat it like a dog. The moose turned away and waded through the freezing water.

Matt mumbled, "Perfect, eh, Rafe? It's all so . . . perfect." Then he let out a long, slow breath.

Rafe could hear the noise of the helicopter before he could see it. Then the noise – *chop, chop, chop* – got louder and louder. Rafe watched the helicopter coming down and landing. He saw men jumping out and coming toward him. *It's like a movie. I'm watching a movie. But I'm in it.*

Hands reached out and picked him up. Voices were shouting and asking questions. Rafe tried to speak but his words were slurred. His head felt so heavy, so tired.

Rafe watched as they hoisted Matt up and inside the helicopter. He felt something warm being wrapped around him. Then he felt the helicopter lift and take them away. Finally he let go and slept. He so needed to sleep.

This time he knew where he was. When he opened his eyes this time, he knew he was in a hospital. He turned his head and saw her.

Diana.

"Hey," she whispered. "Oh my God! You're awake! Oh, Rafe!"

The sight of her made something well up inside him. Rafe knew he was going to cry like a baby. He brought his hand up to his eyes and saw the needles taped to his arm.

Diana sprang from her chair and reached for his hand. He could see her cheeks were wet with tears.

"I didn't want to lose you," Rafe told her. "That helped me survive."

Diana smiled and then a look of anger crossed her face. "But I almost lost you, you . . . you. . . ." She turned away and the word was lost.

He squeezed her hand. "Come on, babe. It's okay now. I'm here and everything's okay."

But Diana didn't meet his eyes and Rafe knew something . . . was not okay.

"Tell me," he begged.

Diana shook her head. "You were lost for five days. You have three broken fingers, a broken ankle and a bunch of cuts that needed stitches and. . . ." Her voice rose. "And you need surgery on one eye and you have broken teeth and. . . ."

"And?"

Diana began to cry. She turned away from him as a doctor came into the room. The doctor told him the rest.

Four toes gone. Amputated. Frostbite. Lucky to be alive.

He turned his face into the pillow and the drugs took over.

When he woke up, his parents were there. There was scolding and yelling mixed with crying and hugging. Rafe would be in the hospital for another two weeks. Only then could he go home and figure out how to live his life.

Matt. The name knifed into his thoughts.

"How is he? Where is he? Can I talk to him?"

His parents both looked away.

Diana sat on the edge of his bed and held his hand again. "He . . . he didn't make it, Rafe. He died beside you, just before they found you. I'm sorry. I'm. . . ."

Rafe yanked his hand away and struggled to sit up. "No! No, you're wrong. He didn't die. He didn't want to die. You're wrong. You've made a mistake. He wanted to live. You've. . . ." But the faces around him told him the truth.

He closed his eyes and heard his parents tiptoe out. Diana laid her hand over his and said nothing.

Confused, Rafe shook his head. As if that could tidy up his thoughts into neat piles. *All of this happened because I tried to save a kid who didn't want to live. But then something happened to him because I chased him. And somehow . . . Matt changed his mind. He wanted to live. And I helped him figure that out.*

Rafe knew he had to believe that. He had to believe that Matt's death wasn't the same death it would have been just days before.

The police would be here soon. And Mr. Longo. There was a lot of explaining to do. Rafe knew he'd be called a stupid idiot several times over. Rafe knew he'd have to relive all the mistakes he'd made.

But at least he could tell them the truth about Matt. What he believed was the truth. Matt had survived, after all. He died, yes. But he died trying to stay alive.

Hostage

by ALEX KROPP

Rob was just making a bank deposit when the robbers burst in. Soon he's one of six hostages down on the floor, trying to keep the trigger-happy bank robbers from losing control. At the end, Rob is the only hostage left – his life hanging by a thread.

Overboard

by E.L. THOMAS

An accident at sea leaves Tanner in a lifeboat with his kid sister and a guy he really despises. The survival of the group depends on their working together. But as the hot sun beats down and the water runs out, their chances don't look good.

Wave

by D.M. OUELLET

Luke and Mai could see the tsunami coming at them, but that didn't give them enough time to get away. When the wave hit, they fought to breathe and fought to reach dry land. And that was only the beginning of the disaster.

Frozen

by LORI JAMISON

Frank and Ray are stranded in the frozen North. Their snowmobile is broken and no one knows where they are. An Arctic storm is coming that can freeze them to death in minutes. The question is simple: how can they survive?

Sharon Jennings is the author of more than sixty books for young people, including the Governor General nominated novel *Home Free*. For HIP, she`s written *Pump, Dancing on the Edge* and six Bat mystery novels, ridiculous stories about Sam and Simon, a couple of 11-year-old boys who effortlessly attract trouble. Visit her website at www.sharonjennings.com

For more information on HIP novels:

High Interest Publishing
www.hip-books.com